Doyley the Dormouse

Keep a look out for those Doyley doors!

Lee Sterrey.

Written by

Lee Sterrey

Illustrated by

Nicola Wyldbore-Smith

ISBN-10: 1506180310
ISBN-13: 978-1506180311

For Jean, Dylan and Amber, whom love Honey Bee Farm adventures.

Inspired by Sean D'Oyley, the carpenter.

Doyley the Dormouse was the best door-maker in town,
He made doors for mouse holes that were perfectly round.

All kinds of mice want a hidden door,
So they needn't worry about being discovered any more.

Doyley's doors fitted so well, that no-one could see,
That behind the door there was a mouse family.

Early one evening, Jessica the mouse,
Visited Doyley at his tree-stump house.

"I need a hidden door will you come and see?
We have just moved to a new place, please follow me."

Doyley stood outside her house and frowned.
"But Jessica" he said, "your door hole is not round.
I'm really not that sure, that I can make a rectangular door."

Jessica replied, "Doyley, you're the best door-maker in town,
You make hidden doors; I know mine's not round.
My family can't move again, it's too late,
We are all getting sleepy and need to hibernate.

I need a door, will you please help me?

Without one, everyone will see my family."

That evening Doyley started to make the door,
And laid out his plans on the workshop floor.

The first door he made was
wonky on the left...

The second door he made was
wonky on the right...

The third door he made was wonky all over and the wrong height!
And although he tried with all his might,
"It is the angles" he said, "that are just not right."

"I am the best door-maker in town,
But how do I make a door that isn't round?

Who will know? Who can I ask?
About how to do this difficult task?"

Pogo the
Pony

Piccolo the
Hound

Snowy the
Cat

Chatty Robin

Doyley thought of the animals on the farm,
Snowy the cat was wise, but he might do harm.

Chatty Robin, he would know best!

Doyley scurried quickly to find the nest.

With a quick flick of his tail he popped in,
And gently woke the Chatty Robin.

The Chatty Robin sleepily said,
"Why are you getting me out of bed?"

"I'm Doyley the Dormouse, the best door-maker in town,
But I have only ever made doors that are perfectly round.
I need your advice, you see,
To help another mouse family…

… a friend of mine, Jessica the mouse,
Needs a rectangle-shaped door for her house."

"The first one I made was wonky on the left.

The second one I made was wonky on the right.

The third one was wonky all over and the wrong height!

And although I've tried with all my might,
It is the angles that are just not right."

"Doyley, you can't be the best door-maker in town,
If the only doors you have made are perfectly round."

Chatty Robin yawned and stretched his claws,
"I know how to make angles right for rectangle doors.

It is your lucky day, it must be fate!
As today, the farmer built a rectangle gate.

While working, the farmer used the 3-4-5 rhyme,
Once you remember it you will be just fine.

To make the perfect right-angle joint…

…take *three* steps right…   *Four*
steps
down…

…And
five
steps
point
to
point."

Doyley followed the rhyme,
And with a large twig he drew the line.

"There is something wrong with this door.
It has three sides, but a rectangle has four."

Robin continued;

"To make a rectangle, all I ask…

… is

take

four

steps

down…

…*three* steps right…

And then you have completed the task!

You have a perfect rectangle, with angles that are right.

Now I'm getting sleepy, so I bid you goodnight!"

Doyley the Dormouse is the best door-maker in town,
He now makes doors of all shapes, not just those that are round.

He made the perfect rectangle door for Jessica's family,

So they were nicely hidden away and no-one could see.

In your garage, shed or house,
You might just have a little mouse.

If you listen carefully, you may hear a squeak,
Or even the scurrying of tiny feet.

So when you wonder, "How did that mouse get in here?"
You now know, that a hidden Doyley door is near!

46023289R00018

Made in the USA
Charleston, SC
11 September 2015